P9-DNM-694

Spunky Little Monkey

by **Bill Martin Jr**
& Michael Sampson

Illustrated by
Brian Won

Scholastic Press • New York

Sleepy Little Monkey

Won't get out of bed.

Mama called the Doctor
And the Doctor said:

"Apple Juice,
Orange Juice,
Gooseberry Pies—

Monkey needs
some exercise!"

Rutabaga,

Rutabaga Sis! Boom! Bah!

POP UP, Monkey! Rah! Rah! Rah!

First you get the rhythm of the head:

Ding-
Dong!

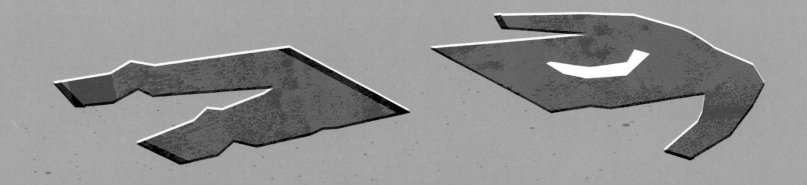

Have you got the rhythm of the head?

Ding-
Dong!

Then you get the rhythm of the hands:

Clap! Clap!

Have you got the rhythm of the hands?

Then you get the rhythm of the feet:

Stomp! Stomp!

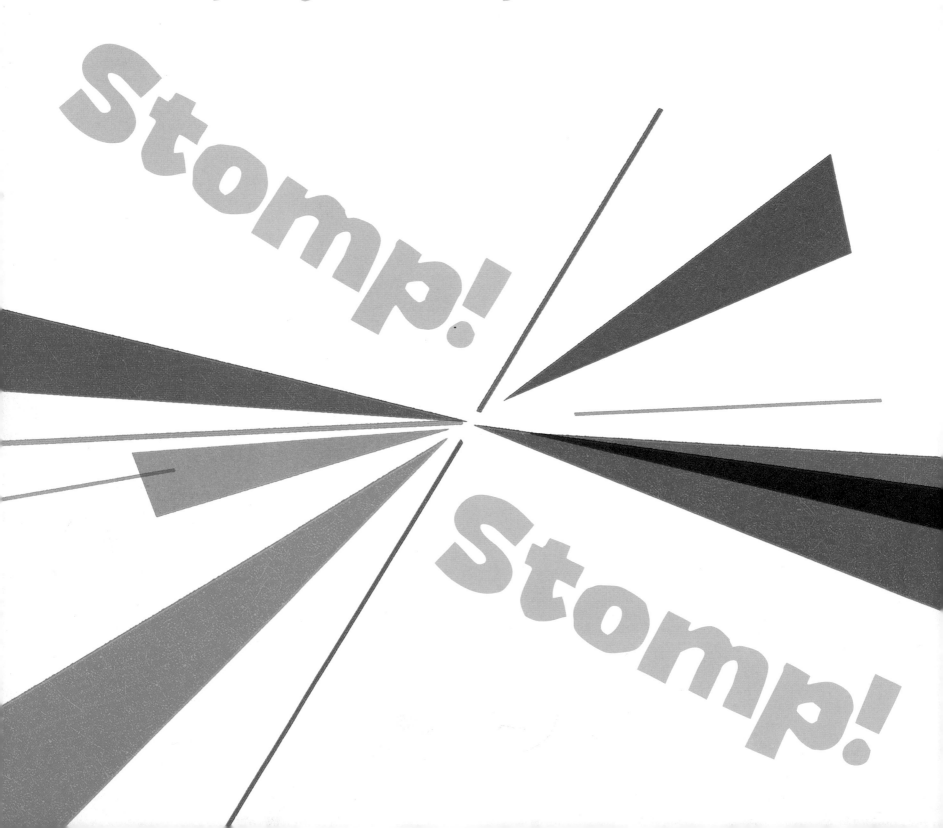

Have you got the rhythm of the feet?

Stomp!

Stomp!

Stomp!

Then you get the rhythm of the hips:

Shake!

Shake!

Have you got the rhythm of the hips?

Put them all together
You'll be feeling so much better:

Do them backward nice and quick,
You'll feel perky, that's the trick!

Shake!
Shake!

Stomp!
Stomp!

Spunky
Little Monkey
Ready
for the day.

Come on, Monkey—

LET'S GO PLAY!

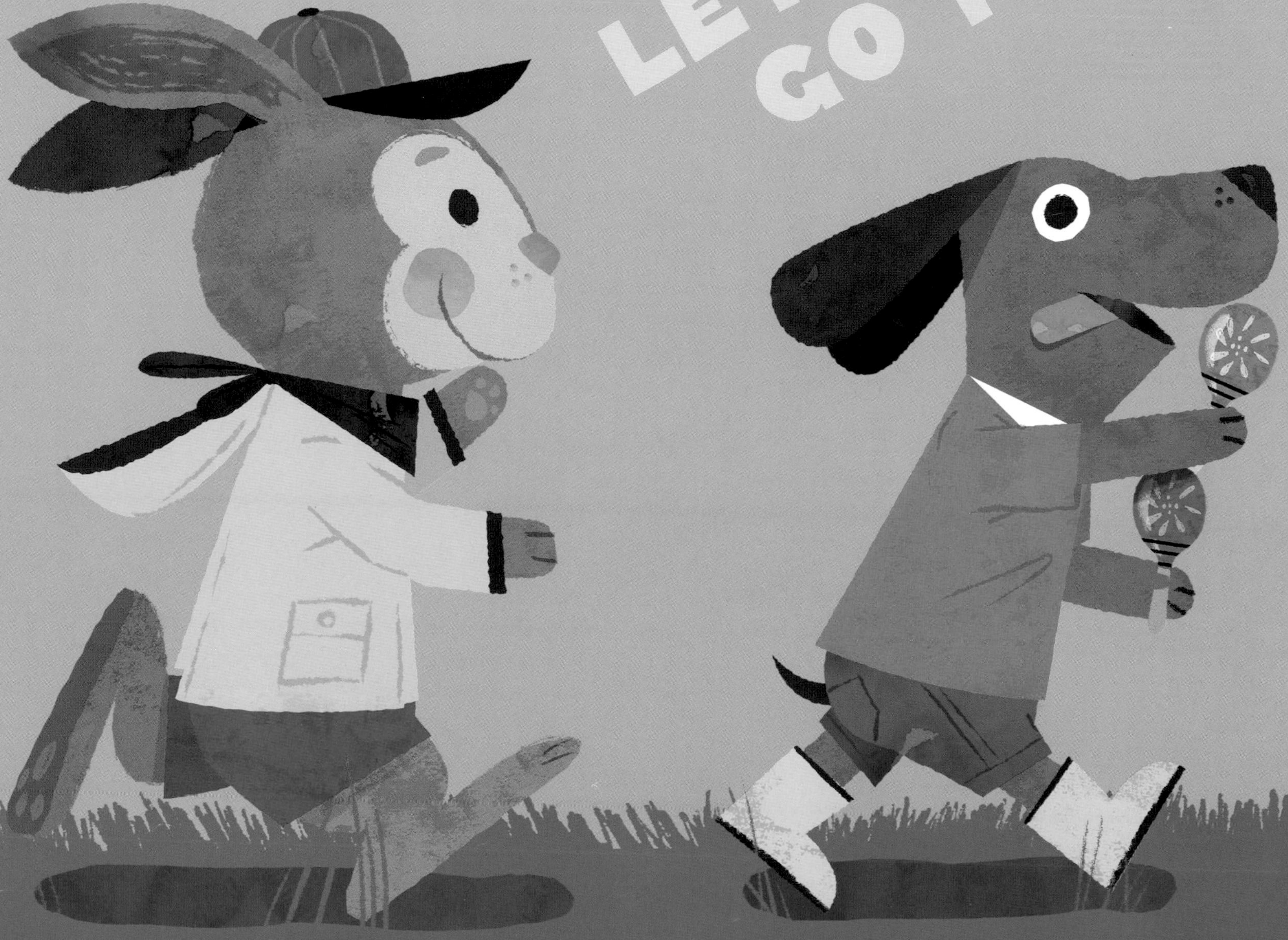

A NOTE FROM MICHAEL SAMPSON

Daily exercise is *very* important.
Not only does it make your arms, legs, lungs, and heart stronger,
it also stimulates brain function and gets little monkeys everywhere ready to learn!

Reading is another form of exercise. It exercises the mind.
We used rhyme, repetition, and art to help your child read this book.
From the first time you read it, your child will want to possess this fun, energetic chant.
In keeping with Bill Martin Jr's philosophy, with subsequent readings
your child will begin chiming in with you.
Soon after, they will read it by themselves as they match the song in their heads
with what is printed on the page.

Reading is not taught, but caught. This book will help your child catch on to reading!

To Michelle Sampson—my
little spunky monkey! —M.S.

For my spunky friend,
Christmas J. —B.W.

Spunky Little Monkey is a modified variation of the popular children's clapping game called "Down Down Baby."

Brian Won's digital illustrations were created in Adobe Illustrator. To get a hand-painted look,
he scans his own washes and acrylic textures along with pen lines, and imports them into Photoshop.
There he applies the blend modes to marry the scanned elements to the vector illustrations.
The text was set in Skizzors Bold and Skizzors Regular.
The display type was set in Skizzors Bold.

Art direction and book design by Marijka Kostiw

Text copyright © 2017 by Michael Sampson • Illustrations copyright © 2017 by Brian Won • All rights reserved. Published by Scholastic Press, an imprint of Scholastic Inc., *Publishers since 1920.* SCHOLASTIC, SCHOLASTIC PRESS, and associated logos are trademarks and/or registered trademarks of Scholastic Inc. • The publisher does not have any control over and does not assume any responsibility for author or third-party websites or their content. • No part of this publication may be reproduced, stored in a retrieval system, or transmitted in any form or by any means, electronic, mechanical, photocopying, recording, or otherwise, without written permission of the publisher. For information regarding permission, write to Scholastic Inc., Attention: Permissions Department, 557 Broadway, New York, NY 10012. • This book is a work of fiction. Names, characters, places, and incidents are either the product of the author's imagination or are used fictitiously, and any resemblance to actual persons, living or dead, business establishments, events, or locales is entirely coincidental. • Library of Congress Cataloging-in-Publication Data • Names: Martin, Bill, 1916-2004, author. | Sampson, Michael R., author. | Won, Brian, illustrator. Title: Spunky little monkey / by Bill Martin Jr & Michael Sampson ; illustrated by Brian Won. Description: First edition. | New York : Scholastic Press, 2017. | Summary: Little monkey will not get out of bed, so the doctor prescribes some exercise, and monkey learns to dance. Identifiers: LCCN 2016009946 | ISBN 9780545776431 (hardcover : alk. paper) Subjects: LCSH: Monkeys—Juvenile fiction. | Dance—Juvenile fiction. | Stories in rhyme. | CYAC: Stories in rhyme. | Monkeys—Fiction. | Dance—Fiction. Classification: LCC PZ8.3.M399 Sp 2017 | DDC [E]—dc23 LC record available at http://lccn.loc.gov/2016009946 •

10 9 8 7 6 5 4 3 2 1   17 18 19 20 21 • Printed in Malaysia   108 • First edition, January 2017